NO
CURVES

GREEN
LIGHT
GO

SAFE
SPEED
35 M.P.H.

PAVED
HIGH-
WAY

SAFETY
ISLAND

TIM *and the* BRASS BUTTONS

by RUTH TOOZE

illustrated by ZHENYA GAY

JULIAN MESSNER, INC. NEW YORK

PUBLISHED BY JULIAN MESSNER, INC.

8 WEST 40TH STREET, NEW YORK 18

PUBLISHED SIMULTANEOUSLY IN CANADA

BY THE COPP CLARK COMPANY, LTD.

COPYRIGHT 1951 BY RUTH TOOZE

PRINTED IN THE UNITED STATES OF AMERICA

To Richard

U. S.753700

Tim and the Brass Buttons

I

WHY the hurry?" asked Mom.

Tim was right on time for breakfast. That did not happen often. Now he was eating fast. He drank the rest of his milk in one gulp and said:

"I want to tell Mike on my way to school."

"Tell Mike what?" asked Dad, as if he didn't know.

"About my puppy, Dad. Mike is my friend and he will be glad I have a puppy."

Mike was the traffic cop at the corner of Oak Street and First Avenue where Tim had to cross every morning on his way to school. He and Tim were friends.

Tim pulled on his sweater. He went to the porch to take a last look at the new

puppy still curled up asleep in his box. Then he ran the two blocks down Oak Street to First Avenue.

Mike stood there, his arms held out for the traffic to go on Oak Street. The lights changed. Then he blew his whistle.

The cars on First Avenue started up.

Tim ran up to Mike, and touched one of the brass buttons on his coat.

"Well, Tim, my boy, you're early this fine morning."

"Mike, I have a surprise. I had to come to tell you."

"Now whatever can that be? You aren't going away somewhere, are you?"

"No, Mike. I have a puppy. He's my own dog."

"Well, well, now isn't that fine! Every boy should have his own dog. What kind is he? And how old is he? Will you be running down here with him after school?"

"Oh, no, Mike, he's just two months old. He's a cocker, a brown one. We got him at the kennel yesterday. He's a good dog, Mike. He has papers."

"Well now, the papers are all right, but I hope he has sharp eyes and a good heart, and is a good dog for you, Tim."

"Oh, he is, Mike. He's the best dog in the world and I'm going to train him."

"Got a name for him yet, Tim?"

"Not yet, Mike. He's brown and I could call him Brownie, and his hair is curly, especially on his ears, so I could call him Curly."

"If you ask me, which you didn't, I'd call him Brownie. That's a good name for

13

a brown cocker. Run along now, Tim. You'll be just on time for school."

As the signal showed green, Mike held up his arms for the traffic to move on First Avenue. Tim ran across the street. He turned and waved to Mike. Then he ran up the block to his school.

"Brownie," he said to himself off and on that morning. "That's a good name for a brown cocker. That's his name. I'll call him that this noon and see if he likes it."

Tim ran all the way home at noon, and went right out to the back porch to see his dog.

"Brownie," he called softly as he knelt down beside the box. The puppy opened his eyes and lifted his head. Tim petted the puppy.

"You like it, don't you, Brownie? Nice Brownie."

Tim ate his lunch quickly, called softly, "Goodbye, Brownie," and started back to school.

"Brownie's O.K.," he called to Mike from the curb as he waited for the green light.

"Good," Mike called back and smiled.

Tim played ball in the empty lot after school, then went to meet Dad's train at the station at 5:15.

"Hi, Dad," he said, as he ran up to his father and took his hand.

"Hi, Tim. How's the pup?"

"He's fine. I'm calling him Brownie."

"Brownie is a good name for a brown cocker."

"That's just what Mike said, Dad. And you know what, Brownie's eyes shine just like Mike's brass buttons. I wish you had buttons like his on your coat."

"I wish I did, Tim. I like them too, but they cost a lot."

Just then they reached home. There was Mom on the porch with Brownie in her arms.

"Isn't he a dear!"

"He's the best dog in the whole world.
I'll give him his supper now." Tim put
some dog meat in Brownie's bowl and
poured a little warm broth over it.
Brownie liked it.

II

The next morning Tim was in a hurry again. He fed Brownie, petted him a little, then ran down the street to school.

Mike was right there at the corner, his brass buttons shining in the sun.

The signal changed and Mike swung around, holding his arms for the traffic to move on First Avenue. Tim ran up to Mike and touched one of his buttons.

"Early again, Tim. Now what?"

"Mike," began Tim slowly.

"Come out with it, boy. Something troubling you?"

"No, not exactly troubling me. Mike, how much do brass buttons cost? An awful lot?"

Mike laughed so hard he shook all over.

"So that's it. Well now, Tim, brass buttons don't cost such a lot of money, but you just can't buy these brass buttons. You have to earn them."

"Earn them? How? I told Dad I liked brass buttons like these. He said he liked them too, but they cost too much."

Mike smiled.

"It's like I said, Tim. It takes more than just money to get buttons like these. It takes a watchful eye, a strong arm and a kind heart, not only to earn them but to keep them."

"I wish I could earn some for my dad and for me when I get big."

"Maybe you can, Tim. A good way to start will be to run along to school now so you're right on time. Tim, my boy, what about Brownie? Is he eating all right?''

"Sure he is, Mike. I fixed his supper and

breakfast and he had his bowl empty in no time. He eats fast. He's growing."

"I can hardly wait to see that dog, Tim."

"I'll bring him down soon," called Tim as the red light changed to green and he ran up First Avenue to Lincoln School.

That night when he met Dad at the 5:15 train he told him about the buttons right away.

"So Mike said you can't buy them just for money, did he? He said you have to earn brass buttons, did he?"

"Yes, Dad, he said you have to earn them with a watchful eye, a strong arm and a kind heart. Does he?"

"What do you think, Tim? Mike is your friend. Does he watch everything at his corner every minute?"

"Every second, Dad. You should see

him. He sees everything. You can't even put your foot down off the curb when you're waiting for the green light. And there are loads of kids to watch."

"Good for Mike."

"And it takes strong arms to hold them out straight and change them with every light. I should think he'd get tired, but he doesn't."

"He's strong. And do you think he has a kind heart, Tim?"

"You bet. He makes the cars wait so the little kids in kindergarten can get across."

"He's a good policeman, Tim. I'm glad he's your friend. I think you could be like him."

"O.K., Dad. I hope I have as much fun as he does. He laughs so hard he shakes. Even his buttons shake, and they shine like anything. I wish we could earn brass buttons, too, Dad."

"Maybe we can, Tim."

III

Tim had a lot of fun in the next months. He had fun in school. He had fun playing in the lot. But he had the most fun with Brownie.

They ran all over the back yard. They
rolled. They tumbled.

30

Ever since Tim started to walk, when Mom couldn't find him right away she would call:

"Tim, Tim, Timothy Tim!

What in the world has become of him?"

Now it seemed as if she had to call it nearly every afternoon. Then Tim would shout back:

"Hi, Mom. Come on, Brownie!" and they would come running from the far corner of the yard.

Tim trained Brownie well. He taught
him to walk on a leash,

to "heel"

to "sit,"

to "stay."

U. S. 753700

Tim showed every new trick to Mike, who grew as proud of Brownie as Tim did. One day Tim took Brownie down to the corner and told him to 'Stay.' Brownie sat still by the curb while Tim ran across to mail a letter for Mom. As he came back he stood near Mike.

"Look, Mike. Doesn't Brownie obey well? He sits right where I tell him to every time I say 'Stay.' Every time."

"He sure is a fine dog, Tim. You're training him well. He has sharp eyes, and that's a fine thing in a dog."

"Like you, Mike. But he can't wear brass buttons."

"Ho! Ho! Now you never can tell."

Tim ran back to the curb. He called, "Come, Brownie," and they started for home. Brownie ran along close beside him.

39

The week before Easter was spring vacation—time for marbles. Tim had lots of marbles. There were marbles in his toy box, in his desk drawers, in his pants' pockets, even in the front hall closet. He collected them all and counted them. 72!

That was good! They were mostly mibs. There was only one shooter and that was not a really good one.

The other boys all had good shooters. Some had clods, those great big shooters. They said you couldn't win unless you shot with a clod.

Tim wished he had some shooters. He had just that old one. He played every day of spring vacation, and won only one game. Brownie sat and watched him.

Dad came home at noon on Saturdays. Tim and Brownie went to meet his train.

Tim told Dad about his marbles.

"I'm getting pretty good. I practice

shooting a lot. But, Dad, I need some good shooters and a couple of clods. Bobby's favorite clod is red. It's his lucky one. He always wins with it. Dad, I need

shooters. I want to win—sometimes, any-how."

"I know how you feel, Tim. You should have some shooters. I once had some. I even had an aggie, but I guess they are lost by now."

"Oh, Dad, a real aggie! They cost an awful lot."

"Yes, they do. I think mine cost five dollars, but I earned the money for it. It was my lucky shooter. I won a lot of games," and Dad laughed as he remembered.

"How about earning your shooters, Tim?"

"How? They cost real money."

Dad laughed again.

"I know," he said. "But, let's see. If Tim's eye watched the wood basket by the fireplace, and filled it every night with his strong arm, that would be kind to Mom. I think we might pay a boy for that, and he could use the money to buy shooters."

"Oh, Dad, that's fine. I'll do it. May I start today?"

"This very afternoon. We'll tell Mom so that she will know what to expect. We'll pay you three cents a basket."

They told Mom about it at lunch. Tim held up his arm and bent it at the elbow to show Mom and Dad how strong it was. You could see his muscle get hard.

Tim and Brownie went out to play after lunch. They found some other boys and played ball for a while over in the lot.

Then they played "Run, Sheep, Run."
Brownie loved that and ran with Tim.

Tim remembered to watch the big clock
in the drugstore window. Five o'clock
came so fast. On the stroke he called
Brownie and they ran home.

He filled the wood basket extra full.

Dad paid him three cents at dinner.

Sunday he filled the basket full. He earned another three cents.

He remembered every afternoon. By Thursday he had fifteen cents. He stopped to tell Mike all about it on the way to school.

"I'll show the shooters to you after school, Mike."

"Fine, Tim. I want to see them."

After school Tim bought a big bright blue clod for ten cents and a swirly blue shooter for five cents. He ran to Mike's corner. When the light changed, he ran up to Mike.

"Look, Mike, aren't they pretty? Blue is my favorite color."

"They sure are, Tim. You'll be winning all the games now."

"I hope so."

Tim showed Mom and Dad his clod and shooter.

"They look like lucky ones," said Dad, as he rolled the clod over the floor.

Tim practiced with the blue clod every day. Soon he really was a good shot. He won many games. The blue clod was his lucky one.

One recess he overheard Bud, the best marble player in second grade, say, "Watch that Tim. He's almost as good as we are and he's only a first grader."

Tim told Mike on the way home from school.

"So you're a good player now, Tim? Even Bud thinks so. Well, well. Use your eyes to watch and aim straight and you'll win."

"I will, Mike. I earned my shooters with a watchful eye and strong arms, you know. Mike, am I just a little bit like you?"

"Well now, you're beginning. You'll have brass buttons yet."

IV

It was a shining Friday morning as
Tim skipped down the front steps with
Brownie at his heels.

Today was the big day, the day of the marble tournament in the school playground after school. Only two first graders made the finals. Tim was one of them.

"Good luck, Tim," called Mom.

"Thanks."

Tim felt happy. He took his bag of marbles out of his pocket and carried it by the string. He and Brownie ran to the corner of Oak Street and First Avenue. They watched Mike standing there with his strong arms out, directing traffic along Oak Street.

Tim began to swing his bag of marbles as he stood there watching for the light to change.

Then it happened. Snap! The string broke.

The marbles rolled into the street, Tim

after them, Brownie after Tim. The lights changed. Brownie barked. He barked louder and louder.

Mike swung about. He saw what had happened. He blew his whistle and held up his strong arms to hold back the cars. One car, watching for the signal to change, had started forward but slammed on the brakes and stopped three feet from Tim.

"Tim, Tim, go back to the curb. Let those marbles go."

Tim went back and sank down on the curb.

Mike let the signals direct the traffic and ran to him.

"You're all right, Tim? All right? Whatever made you run against the light? You know better. Brownie saved your life,

Tim. Brownie barked so loud, I heard and held back the cars. Oh, Tim," and Mike bent over him to make sure he was all right.

"I'm sorry, Mike," came a weak little voice from Tim. "I'm sorry. I was thinking of the marble tournament. Then the string broke. All I thought of was getting my marbles. I forgot all about lights."

"But, Tim, you can't ever forget lights, not ever. Don't you remember, you earn the buttons with a watchful eye?"

"I know, Mike. I'm sorry I forgot."

"That's not enough, Tim. You must not forget," said Mike, as he fumbled with one of his brass buttons, and gave it a quick jerk.

"Look, Tim. We are tying this brass button on Brownie who earned it with a watchful eye, a strong bark and a kind heart. Good Brownie, good boy."

"Oh, Mike, thank you. Brownie is wagging his tail. That means 'Thank you.' He earned a button before I did, Mike. Run home now, Brownie. Run home and show them your button. Home."

Brownie obeyed Tim and ran home.

"Mike?"

"Yes, Tim, what is it?"

"Mike, do you think I'll ever earn a brass button?"

"Sure you will, Tim. But you mustn't forget to remember."

"Oh, I won't, Mike. I won't forget to remember." Tim picked up his marbles.

The green light was on. He ran up the hill to school.

Mike went back to his place on the corner, his brass buttons shining in the sun, one corner of his coat flapping where a button was missing.